W9-AAF-324

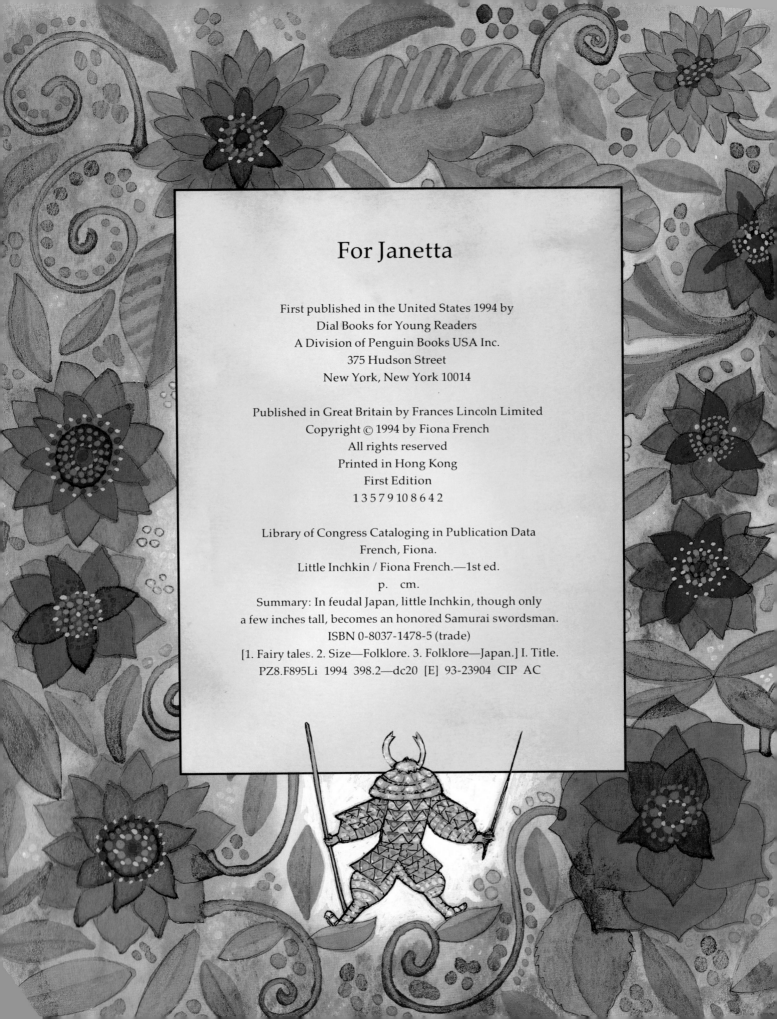

For Janetta

First published in the United States 1994 by
Dial Books for Young Readers
A Division of Penguin Books USA Inc.
375 Hudson Street
New York, New York 10014

Published in Great Britain by Frances Lincoln Limited
Copyright © 1994 by Fiona French
All rights reserved
Printed in Hong Kong
First Edition
1 3 5 7 9 10 8 6 4 2

Library of Congress Cataloging in Publication Data
French, Fiona.
Little Inchkin / Fiona French.—1st ed.
p. cm.
Summary: In feudal Japan, little Inchkin, though only
a few inches tall, becomes an honored Samurai swordsman.
ISBN 0-8037-1478-5 (trade)
[1. Fairy tales. 2. Size—Folklore. 3. Folklore—Japan.] I. Title.
PZ8.F895Li 1994 398.2—dc20 [E] 93-23904 CIP AC

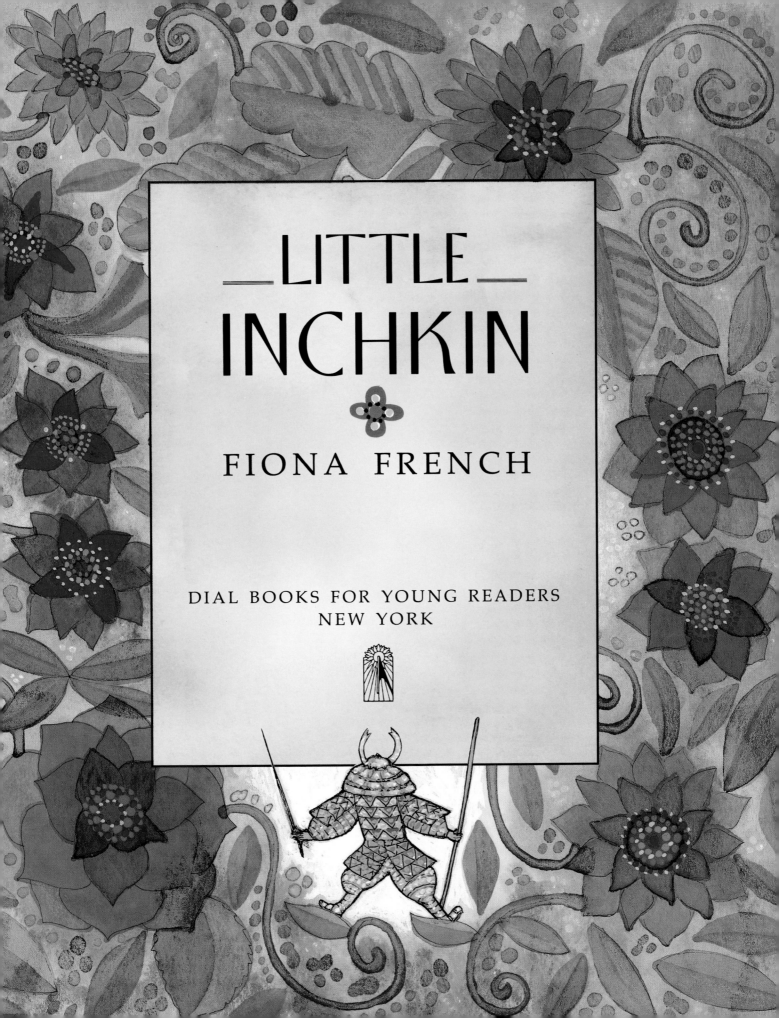

LITTLE INCHKIN

FIONA FRENCH

DIAL BOOKS FOR YOUNG READERS
NEW YORK

Long ago in old Japan, Hana lived with her husband Tanjo in a small house near a temple. They both longed for a child.

One day Hana and Tanjo took gifts to the temple and laid them before the great Buddha. "Please give me a child," Hana whispered. "Girl or boy, plain or pretty—I would love it just the same."

A voice answered her, "Return home, Hana. Your wish has been granted."

Not long afterward Hana had a beautiful baby boy—but he was the smallest child ever seen. "He is only as big as a pea-pod!" she cried. "All of our neighbors will make fun of me."

She and Tanjo named the tiny boy Inchkin. Although they took great care of him, they did not love him, for they were ashamed to have a son hardly bigger than a thumb.

Children stared at Inchkin, and would not let him join their games. So all alone he played, and dreamed of one day becoming a tall, brave swordsman.

The years passed, and Inchkin became very brave. He was kind and clever too. But still he was no bigger than a lotus flower, and this made him sad, for he longed with all his heart to be big like other men.

One day he could bear it no longer.

"I will go out into the wide world to find my fortune," he told his mother. "And maybe I will find a way to grow as tall as other people," he sighed to himself.

His mother wished him well as he set out carrying a bundle of rice-balls and plums, but in her heart she was relieved to see him go.

At once Inchkin set about learning to defend himself. With a sharp sword made from a needle and millet straw, and armor of beetles' wings, he fought off crickets and bumblebees, and even a big mouse. He became a skilled swordsman.

One afternoon he climbed into a tiny boat
made from a nutshell and sailed out to the big
river.

A storm whipped up the waves and a shoal
of flying fish almost overturned his boat. But
Inchkin held on tight and beat them off with
his sword. The next morning the sky bright-
ened, the sun shone through the clouds,
and a light breeze swept his little boat
through the city and beyond.

Suddenly he felt himself lifted out of the water and passed from hand to hand, until a voice far above him asked, "Little warrior, who are you?"

"I am called Inchkin," he cried, flourishing his tiny sword in the air. "I am one of the best swordsmen in Prince Sanjo's land."

"And I am Prince Sanjo," said the voice. "Let us see just how good a swordsman you are."

Inchkin now became an officer in the prince's guard. Tales of his bravery spread far and wide, for in a single hour he rid the royal rice-store of rats and the royal kitchens of cockroaches.

Prince Sanjo was impressed by his chivalrous new officer, and one day he summoned him.

"Now, little warrior, I have a special task for you. My daughter is traveling to a temple far away in the mountains, and she has asked if you will guard her on her journey."

Inchkin bowed, and took his place of honor in the princess's carriage.

The next day the princess's carriage arrived
at the ancient temple. Night was falling, and
shadows were flitting among the trees. Inchkin
stood on the princess's shoulder to guard her
more closely. Suddenly two fiery demons who
had strayed down from the mountains blocked
their way.

The princess went pale and trembled with fear, but Inchkin gripped his tiny sword, ready to defend her with his life. He drew himself up to his full height.

"Come any closer, and I will kill you!" he cried.

The two demons were astonished. One of them loomed over him. "You are very frightening," the demon sneered. "Why, I could swallow you in one gulp!" He reached out to pop Inchkin into his mouth.

Inchkin lunged at him with his sharp sword.

"*Aieee!*" cried the demon, and backed away. Inchkin jumped to the ground, yelling a fierce battle-cry.

Before the other demon knew what was going on, the little warrior climbed up his leg, sprang onto his shoulder, and stabbed him hard in the nose. The demon howled with pain, and in a flash both spirits fled.

At that moment the temple bells began to ring, and as each pure note rang out across the vast mountains, Inchkin felt himself growing bigger and bigger. The Lord Buddha was rewarding him for his bravery by granting him his dearest wish: From now on he would be as tall as other men.

When the princess, who had grown fond of Inchkin, saw that he was now a handsome warrior, her heart filled with joy.

Together they returned to the palace. Prince
Sanjo gladly gave them his blessing and they
were married with great rejoicing. Inchkin
welcomed Hana and Tanjo to the wedding. At
first they were deeply ashamed, but kindhearted
Inchkin forgave them for their earlier coldness to
him, and at the wedding they were very proud—
for small or tall, their warrior son was now the
most honored samurai swordsman in the land.